Busy Bee an Endangered Meadow

Paul Noël

By the same author:

Brown Bear's Big Day Out

Clever Dad and the Pirate Ship

Clever Dad and the Space Rocket

Island Spider

The Lost Marble

Junagarh Books

Published by Junagarh Media

Contact address:

info@junagarhmedia.co.uk

www.junagarhmedia.co.uk

Part 1

Old Oak meadow was a beautiful place, no matter what time of the year,

although in the spring, summer and autumn seasons, it looked its best. In

the spring, leaves returned to the trees, flowers bloomed and plants grew.

More creatures could be seen as those hibernating in winter woke up.

Large numbers of birds that had spent the winter in the south, now

migrated north, to spend the warmer seasons in the green landscape of the

meadow and the surrounding countryside.

A road ran alongside the flat land at the top of the meadow and from there,

it sloped gently down to a small stream. Cows sometimes grazed on the

meadow's grass and many people walked through it. Walkers came from a

nearby village and some of them brought their dogs. Others arrived from

further away to enjoy the natural beauty of it and the surrounding area.

There were usually more people during the weekends and the summer

holidays but on most days, even in winter, there were still visitors to be

seen in it.

The beautiful meadow was alive with colours, smells and sounds that

changed as the seasons did. In winter the colours were more subdued and it

was a quieter place. As the weather became warmer the meadow teemed with new life and it was filled with a rising crescendo of sounds and vibrant colours. There were so many types of trees, plants and flowers and these attracted lots of different insects, birds and animals from far and wide.

In one of the old oak trees a bee hive could be found and Beatriz the honey bee lived here. Winter had been a time for the bees to all huddle together to keep the hive and themselves warm. Now winter had been shaken off they returned to their work of pollinating flowers and collecting nectar. Beatriz, as always, was excited and ready early for the spring when it arrived.

Beatriz or Bea to everyone who knew her, was a good worker bee, and during the warmer months she collected lots of nectar, much more than the other bees. The Queen Bee was always very pleased with Bea as she worked the hardest out of all of them in the hive. Bea enjoyed her work as there were so many flowers to take a nectar drink and collect the pollen from. This allowed the bees to make more than enough honey to keep themselves fed during the cold winter months. During this cold time of the year the bees lived off the honey that they had made and stored during the warmer seasons.

Bea disliked the cold days of winter the most, especially if it rained or snowed, because of being stuck inside and not allowed out. She much preferred to be outside working and playing. Although the bees were very snug, warm and protected against the weather in the strong old oak tree, Bea was not happy on winter days when she could not leave the hive. She, like the other bees, at this time of year, spent her time, vibrating her wings and moving about inside the hive to keep the Queen, herself and the others warm.

Sometimes, even in the spring and autumn, there could be days that kept Bea from leaving the hive because of the coldness of the rain and the strength of the wind. Thankfully for her, there were not too many days like

3

these and most of the time Bea could do what she loved to do. The rain, of course, was very necessary and on the days when it had been raining the meadow would look very different afterwards. Once the sun had come out again from behind the clouds, everything seemed fresh and clean and more plants and flowers grew than before. Bea would smile to herself thinking this was the true meaning of the term 'spring clean'!

Bea loved to fly, especially, during the longest and warmest days of summer. She did not just fly to and from flowers like many of the other bees, who just thought of their work as chores. She liked to play and be an aerial acrobat. Bea danced around the flowers and often went careering through them at high speed. At other times Bea dropped from the sky, like a stone, and then pulled herself up sharply. On a few occasions she came near to making a crash landing on a flower but happily never did. Bea had a lot of fun flying and being free.

The summer days were wonderful for Bea as she could work and play for many hours. She was always the first to leave the hive, when the sun rose in the sky, and regularly the last one back when the shadows were long from the sinking sun. Bea often tried to race other bees out of the hive in the morning but most of the time the other bees did not want to know. Even though they were not like their relations the Bumble Bees, her fellow bees were much keener on just bumbling out of the hive than rushing off to work like she did every day that she could.

"We know that we aren't Bumble Bees Bea, but if we all raced about like you, we might become known as Racy Bees or Speedy Bees," several of the other bees had said to her.

She had been told this on different occasions when her attempts to organise early morning races and competitions had failed. Because of this Bea could be seen zooming out of the hive on her own on most mornings. Sometimes she arrived so early that some of the flowers that she visited were still closed! Jokingly, Bea could be seen knocking on the outside and asking them to open up. The poor sleepy flowers could occasionally be a bit grumpy, but sooner or later they would open up their petals and eventually let her in.

In the early mornings, with the sun still low in the sky, Bea also had another problem because sometimes she did not see the cobwebs that the spiders had recently made. Not that they stopped her, usually she went crashing through them. The unfortunate spider, whose web it was, would be none too happy with Bea for damaging so much of his or her time consuming and hard work. If sometimes she became tangled up in the web, the spider would chase her, and she would have to fly away quickly. Bea's eagerness caused her other difficulties. On more than one occasion, she had come back very wet after having left the hive too early following a rain shower. Rain drops are quite big compared to the size of a bee and she sometimes felt the 'splosh' of one of them after flying out before the rain had stopped. Sometimes, from not being careful enough when flying around a flower that was still dripping wet, after it had rained, she also got soaked. She did not take water seriously enough, even though it could make her flying erratic and her wings heavy, and this slowed her down. Luckily for Bea not many creatures wanted to eat bees, so flying more slowly while she dried out was not too much of a problem.

Bea had been called a clever bee as she knew all about flowers and the work that she had to do each day. Flowers attracted bees by producing nectar that the bees drank and then made into honey in the hive. The flowers also made pollen that the bees picked up on their hairs as they took a free drink. They then carried the pollen to the next flowers that they visited and would leave some of it on them. Part of the bees' work involved pollinating the flowers in exchange for drinking their nectar. They helped the flowers and the flowers helped them. Most of the other bees just flew randomly from one flower to another, cross pollinating anything, so sometimes the pollen was wasted. Not so Bea however, who knew her plants and flowers so well she could almost paint the meadow from memory. She had worked out that, if she mixed pollen from a white flower with that of a red one from the same species, then the next year pink flowers would grow in the same place. A wise old bee who lived in the hive had once called her 'Mendel' after some famous person. Bea had always meant to find out who that person was but never did as she was the original busy bee.

Part 2

So began one of Bea's favourite, long days of summer. The night had been a little chilly as she waited for the sun to rise higher in the sky before leaving the hive. All around her the other worker bees were still sleeping, stretching, yawning, or grooming their wings. Bea, ready as usual, raring to go, had already warmed her wings up with her early morning exercises. She went to yoga classes for bees and this saved her time when she prepared herself for flying. Outside, the sun rose slowly in the light blue sky. Only a few long and thin clouds were to be seen, their colours changing with the rays of the climbing sun. Bea raced out of the hive as she always did.

"Good morning everyone!" Bea shouted cheerfully as she left.

All she heard, as on other days, were bees mumbling and giving half asleep replies, since most bees are not at their best at that time of the morning. Bea started as she always did with an inspection of the meadow to see if there had been any changes during the night. Not that there often were, apart from if there had been a major storm with high winds, and these happened more often during the winter. On this morning, Bea was a little surprised, she was flying along steadily when she started to feel the air move as if it had suddenly become very windy.

"Good morning," a bird called Victoria said as she flew alongside Bea.

"Whoa, good morning Victoria," Bea replied as she fought to steady herself and tried to remain flying straight.

Most of the birds were friendly enough, but few of them seemed to realise how much larger they were than Bea and the other bees, or how much turbulence in the air they caused when they flew too close.

"I think that there are some nice new yellow flowers coming out near the stream this morning," suggested the very helpful Victoria.

"Thank you," Bea replied, "is that where you are going for your berries?"

"Yes, I am, there should be some nicely ripe and juicy ones this morning, but you have to be early."

"I'm glad to hear somebody else say that too because I always say that if you leave it too late then the best food of the day can be missed."

"Yes, as you know, one of my relatives once said that it is the early bird that catches the worm. I myself prefer berries. I have never quite understood why anyone would like to eat worms," replied Victoria.

"See you later at the stream for breakfast," Bea answered as Victoria flew on towards the stream.

Bea decided to fly behind Victoria, she found it a bit of a bumpy flight but was used to it having followed other birds before. Beneath her, she saw two cows starting to munch the grass. A little further on a tent had been put up, but the campers had not come out yet; they were a bit late, she thought, as it was such a beautiful day to be up early. As Bea approached the stream she saw the yellow flowers and flew down to take a closer look. They were so pretty that she circled around, admiring them before choosing one to drink from. Bea also noticed some red flowers appearing that day but decided that they could wait until later. She remembered these from the previous year and that they differed a little to the other flowers.

The nectar of the yellow flower smelt wonderful and tasted fresh. Bea picked up some pollen on her hairs as she drank. When she took off, she looked around for another yellow flower close by. She found another of the same species and flew the short distance to it. Here she took another drink and exchanged the pollen that she carried.

Flying across the meadow Bea repeated this several times, with different types of flowers, until she had collected enough nectar before returning to the hive. Bees had to visit a very large number of flowers to collect enough nectar needed to make honey. It was very hard work and required a lot of effort. As she returned from her first foraging some of her fellow worker bees were only just leaving and streaming out. Once she had given her

nectar to other worker bees in the hive she left for the second time that day.

"Well done Bea, your hard work as usual is much appreciated," the Queen

Bee said delightedly as Bea raced out of the hive.

"All in a day's work," she replied with a big, happy smile.

"It's nice to see somebody leading by example," the Queen Bee added.

On this flight, Bea decided to inspect the area and look at the flowers near

the entrance of the meadow, between one of the hedges and the road. There

were often some interestingly different plants to be seen around here.

When she reached the gate she saw a man busily putting up a new notice

on a new wooden post. Strange, thought Bea, why was there a need for another notice? The first notice already in place asked visitors not to make fires, not to leave any rubbish, to always close the gate and not to let their dogs scare farm or other animals. So what was this new notice all about?

Bea busied herself collecting nectar and exchanging pollen from flowers while the man finished putting his notice up. After he had climbed back in his van and driven off, Bea hovered near the notice to read what it said. The words did not make much sense to her, they included 'planning permission', 'construct houses', 'access road' and 'service facilities'. Besides these were many other words, some of which she did know, but a lot that she had not come across before. Bea decided that she had better go back and ask the Wise Old Bee, who very rarely flew very far these days, what they meant. She knew that these words could be important and she was a little worried. The Wise Old Bee might want to read this new notice herself.

Back at the hive Bea found the Wise Old Bee and recited the words that she could remember having read. The Wise Old Bee became more animated than Bea had seen her in a long time.

"Are you sure that those are the words you read Bea?" asked the Wise Old Bee, looking very serious and concerned.

"Yes, there were others but I don't remember them, is it something important?"

"Unfortunately it is," replied the worried looking Wise Old Bee, "it means that there are some people who want to rip apart the meadow and build houses on it. Instead of all the flowers, plants, trees and bushes that you see today they will put their flat, dull, green grass, all over it."

"Oh no!" gasped a surprised Bea.

"Yes, I'm afraid that is what is most likely going to happen. This old oak tree that we live in might get chopped down. Most of the birds, the plants, the trees, the insects and the animals could all disappear, and many of our friends won't survive."

"What can we do about it?" Bea asked in a sad little voice.

"I don't think we can do much against the builders constructing these houses. I had better fly with you and read the notice myself," said the Wise Old Bee, and then added, "There is one small hope."

"What is it?" enquired a curious Bea.

"Well, if a rare or endangered species were to be discovered here then they would not be allowed to build on it. All nature is fragile when it comes into contact with people but they do regard some parts of it as very special sometimes and they try to protect it."

"What is a rare or endangered species?" enquired Bea.

"It is a species of plant, tree, animal, insect, bird, fish, or amphibian which isn't found anywhere else or in only a few other places."

"How do we find one of those?" an excited Bea asked.

"I'm not sure," replied the Wise Old Bee frowning, "I just don't know but we need to find one and find one soon. Take me to the notice so that I can read it properly. Don't fly too fast; remember I'm not as young as you."

They both left the hive, the Wise Old Bee huffing and puffing as she did so. Bea wondered how they could fly so slowly without falling out of the sky. It took quite some time to get to the gate, with the Wise Old Bee having to stop on several plants and bushes along the way for a rest.

At last they arrived at the entrance and the Wise Old Bee set about reading the notice, carefully, including the very small print at the bottom. It was very bad news for all of the living things in the area. They did not have long, the application to build houses had already been placed before the council. Because it was just another meadow there might not be anyone who was prepared to contest the planning application.

"From what I have read, we might have to move the hive very quickly Bea," said the Wise Old Bee, "we don't have long."

"What would one of these rare or endangered species look like?" asked Bea.

"As I said I really don't know," replied the Wise Old Bee, deep in thought. She continued, "But they would somehow be different to what we see in the meadow and what is in the surrounding countryside."

"Oh, but everything looks so different around here, how could we tell?" persisted Bea anxiously.

"I'm sorry," the now very worried looking Wise Old Bee said, "but I'm not sure if any of us know that."

Bea had a flash of inspiration and asked, "What if we made a new species up?"

"What do mean by make one up, how could we do that?" said the Wise Old Bee looking very mystified.

"Well," said Bea, her mind racing, "I found some interesting plants down by the stream this morning. I remember them from last summer. We could use the sticky red pollen from those flowers to colour some of our yellow hairs red. Then we could fly about in front of the visitors that come to walk here until they see us. Then they might think we were a new species of bee."

"Brilliant thinking Bea," said an excited Wise Old Bee, "at least it may give us some time to find a real rare or endangered species. We must go and discuss this with the Queen. The meadow, our homes and the lives of all the living things in it may rely on that thought."

Part 3

The Wise Old Bee seemed to forget her age and they flew back to the hive in half the time that it had taken them to get to the gate. On their arrival they went to see the Queen to explain everything that Bea had discovered. The Wise Old Bee started by explaining about the notice that they had read together.

"We don't have much time to find a rare or endangered species but if we don't, then we must move and find a new home for the hive," she gasped, as she tried to breathe and speak at the same time. "But Bea has come up with an idea that might give us a chance to stay here for at least a while."

"Please tell me about it," said the very concerned Queen.

"Certainly. Some of the bees would have to go out each morning and cover themselves in the sticky red pollen of a tall red flower that grows down by the stream," replied Bea. "Once disguised, the bees would then fly past as many people coming to the meadow as possible so that they start to see red bees. Hopefully, one or more of these visitors will report seeing a new species of bee. When the bees have finished for the day and on their way back home, they would need to leave the pollen on the red flowers as they do normally when they pollinate them. Then they must brush off any that remains so that they are never seen returning to this hive as red bees."

"Why do they need to do this before coming back here?" asked the Queen.

"Because we need to keep everyone guessing, they must never find the hive, they only need to know that it is somewhere in the meadow."

"Oh, I see!" said the Queen.

"That may hopefully give us enough time to find a real species that is either rare or endangered. Once found the meadow would be protected and not built on," the Wise Old Bee added.

"How are we going to find such a species?" asked the Queen.

"The best way, I believe," said the Wise Old Bee, "is for us to ask anyone who will listen to us, the birds, the animals and the insects, even the fish and the amphibians, if they know of one. This idea may only work with the cooperation of all those living here around us."

"Then I am going to ask all the bees to pass the message on to all our friends when they are out foraging for nectar," replied the Queen, "How many other bees do you want to disguise with red pollen?"

"Let me go out on my own at first," Bea suggested, "there are some people camping in the meadow, so I can find out how they react to seeing a red bee."

"That's a very good plan," a smiling Queen replied, "but Bea you must be careful not to get caught."

"I shall be very careful," she answered assuredly.

Bea left the hive; she was very excited as she did so. She remembered exactly where the red flowers were from earlier in the day and flew straight there in no time. The flowers produced a type of pollen that stuck quite well to her hairs as it was a bit more sticky than most. She thought that with the right movements, she should be able to make most of her yellow hairs look red.

Bea found a newly opened red flower near the stream and went inside. Instead of collecting nectar, she buzzed about and took great care to make her yellow hairs rub up against the stamen of the flower. Soon there were only a few of her yellow hairs left to be seen. Bea had become disguised as a red and black honey bee.

She then left the flower and flew to the edge of the water to check and see what she looked like. Her reflection in a quiet part of the stream convinced her that she could fool anyone with this disguise, as long as they did not catch her. She took off. Flying over to the tent that she had seen earlier that day she saw that the two campers had woken up and risen and were sitting outside. She tried zooming back and forth without going too close but they were talking to each other and did not notice her. She decided that she must fly closer to get their attention.

There were some daisies and dandelions near the feet of the two campers. Bea landed on one of them, but they still did not appear to see her. She moved from one flower to another trying to make as loud a buzzing sound as possible. Finally, one of the two saw her.

"Wow, look at that, a red bee, that's unusual," exclaimed David, the young man.

"Where?" replied his companion, a young woman called Jessica.

"There, look, look!" he said excitedly, pointing with his finger at Bea.

"Quick Jess, get your camera and take a photograph."

Jessica hurried into the tent to get her camera with its special lens for taking close-up photographs of subjects such as flowers and bees. Bea buzzed around the other end of the tent while she did this. David took his

phone out of his pocket and took several pictures of Bea himself.

"Hurry, she might fly away and we might miss the opportunity of a good

photograph," said David.

"I'm coming," replied Jessica.

As Jessica rushed out of the tent with her camera, Bea put on a

performance by darting back to the small group of daisies and dandelions.

Jessica took several photographs and when she stopped, David moved

closer to examine Bea. It seemed unlikely that he would try to catch her but

Bea was not going to take any chances. She took off and circled the tent a couple of times before leaving and making sure that they followed the direction of her flight. She stopped at a safe distance and looked back to see where Jessica and David were. This was to make sure that they were not chasing after her to find out where she went.

"We need to upload these pictures on to the internet and send them to our friends and to some of the newspapers. I'm sure that there could be a lot of interest in them," Jessica said to David.

"Yes, you are right," he replied.

Bea waited and then noticed that both of them had got on their bicycles and cycled off. She hoped that they were going to the nearby village to spread the word of their exciting discovery. Once they disappeared from her view she flew to the stream and in the opposite direction to the hive. Here she deposited what pollen she could on another red flower and then spent time brushing the rest off. This proved difficult to do and Bea returned to the hive still with a slightly red tinge. She recounted her story to a rapt audience of the Queen, the Wise Old Bee and the other bees in the hive, who were all waiting for her to return.

"We have also been very busy while you have been away Bea," said the Queen, after she had finished her tale, "we have been asking everyone whether they know of any rare or endangered species."

"Have any been found yet?" enquired Bea hopefully.

"No, everyone thinks they are very ordinary and they feel that they have lots of relations living here in the meadow and outside of it. They also believe that none of the plants or trees are very special either."

"We must continue to keep searching then and hopefully find one before our little disguise is discovered," replied Bea.

Bea and the other bees returned to collecting nectar. Some bees flew around just to see if there were any more visitors but it was a very quiet day and no one else came. As nobody else visited there was no need for Bea to be disguised again that day as a red bee. The two campers returned but they did not need further convincing. They were already telling everyone they knew through their social media contacts about what they had seen. There was nothing more that the bees could do that day except wait and see and go about their normal work.

Part 4

The next day, as the first rays of light started to spread across the meadow, Bea left the hive and flew to the first group of red flowers that she could find. She turned herself once more into the red bee and then went out to see what was happening with the couple that were camping not far from the stream. Bea flew around and visited some flowers as there did not seem to be much activity and she could not see the campers. She loitered close by performing some loops around the tent. Eventually Jessica and David emerged and started to prepare their breakfast. They checked their phones while doing so to see what updates they had received.

"Have you seen how many times those photographs that you took of that red bee have been viewed Jess?" David asked with great enthusiasm.

"Yes, amazing, we have never had so many hits with our images before this," answered Jessica.

"It's not very often anyone gets to take photos like the ones that you did yesterday," replied David.

They ate their breakfast and afterwards checked their emails. There were many comments and conversations about Jessica's photographs. When they had finished David cycled to the local village shop, returning fifteen minutes later with a newspaper.

"Look at this!" he said with a big smile as Jessica poured him another cup of tea.

"That photograph came out really well in the newspaper. It's a shame that it is only a local paper that has decided to print it," Jessica replied.

"I checked and it wasn't in any of the national ones," said David.

As they sat reading the paper together, Bea crept up behind them to get a look at it as well. A very large photograph of her, one of the ones that Jessica had taken filled a large part of one of the pages. A large and bold headline above the image read:

"New Species Of Bee Discovered?"

It was Bea's turn to be very excited and she wanted to return to the hive and tell everyone, but first she had to make sure that the two campers saw her again, which she did. Secondly, everyone had agreed that before returning to the hive that no bees should be disguised in red. Bea flew towards the stream; the couple watching her disappear into the distance.

With great haste she deposited her pollen on another red flower and brushed most of the rest off.

What Bea was unaware of, however, was that some property developers, some individuals working at the local council, and a large number of others had also seen her photograph on the internet and in the local newspaper. Bea had no idea at this time of what she had actually started.

When she arrived back at the hive it was time to start the next phase of the plan. Before this, she had to explain about the articles and photographs, in the newspaper and on the internet, to all the bees eagerly waiting for her.

"So what do we do next?" asked the Queen.

"Well," said Bea, "the Wise Old Bee and I thought that some of the bees should fly around and be near the gate all the time. Then they can inform us when anyone comes into the meadow. As more red bees need to be seen, I think we need another five volunteers to don the disguise to look like I do. Then we can put on a show and be seen by anyone else that visits here."

"I'm sure that this should be easy to arrange," the Queen replied, "can I have some volunteers to become disguised as red bees please?"

Everyone was very excited by now; you could say there was a real buzz about the hive. They had more volunteers than they required, so Bea, the Queen and the Wise Old Bee selected the five most experienced and fastest flyers to be disguised as the red bees. It would not be good for any of the bees to be captured on this risky mission and they needed their best bees for the job.

"Is there any further news on finding a real rare or endangered species?" enquired a hopeful Bea.

"I'm afraid not," the Wise Old Bee replied, "we are still searching. We have more cooperation in this meadow than ever before but so far we have no possible candidates."

"Then let us see then if this plan of ours is enough to save our home," said a concerned Bea.

Bea explained the task to the five chosen bee volunteers. As they left to go and find their disguise, some other bees left for the meadow's gate to keep watch and then alert Bea's team when other people arrived. Her group of bees flew to the red flowers and got themselves ready. When they had all finished preparing themselves they looked very different from when they had started. They hid in a patch of mixed tall plants so as not to be seen just by chance. Time passed and later, a bee called Stephanie, who had been keeping watch on the gate, flew hurriedly over to them.

"Two men have arrived and one of them is carrying a large camera," she reported, "and they were walking over to the tent."

"Right," said Bea decisively. She turned to one of the red bees, "Amelia, you come with me, the rest of you stay here until we call you. We don't want them thinking that there are a large number of us just yet."

Bea, Amelia and Stephanie flew towards the tent of the couple camping. The new arrivals, a reporter and a photographer for the local newspaper were talking to Jessica and David when the three of them arrived. Bea told the other two bees how to get this group's attention.

Stephanie, without a disguise, flew over and landed on the same daisies and dandelions that Bea had perched on yesterday. The four people saw her but did not take any real notice. Then Bea joined Stephanie and Jessica caught site of her.

"Look, there's one of the red bees," Jessica pointed excitedly at Bea.

The others turned to see where Jessica was pointing. As John the reporter turned to look at Bea, Amelia flew into his line of vision, flying over the tent and settling on a tall flower on the other side. They all turned to follow Amelia and Bea took off. Ben the photographer checked his camera and strode over to where Amelia pretended to drink nectar. He took several photographs of her.

"That's amazing! I have never seen anything like this before and I expect a lot of experts are going to want to visit the area now," said Ben.

Amelia joined Bea and Stephanie at a safe distance and they watched what happened next. The group of four people talked about what they had all now seen for a few minutes and when finished the reporter and photographer walked back towards the gate. Stephanie flew back to the gate behind them to join the other bees keeping watch. Bea and Amelia joined the other four red bees and waited for the next visitors to arrive.

Another hour passed and this time another bee, Emily, who had been watching the gate, approached Bea's group to report that two men were standing outside and talking. The two men were from the local council. Bea assembled her whole team this time and led them to the entrance of the meadow. She made sure that they all remained inside the boundary at various distances from the gate. As the two men appeared deep in conversation, but were still just outside, Bea flew across their line of vision getting closer and closer until one of them noticed her.

"Well I never," exclaimed one of the men to the other with a raised voice. "Oh yes, and there's another," said the other man pointing at Amelia, "we should go in and see if we can see some more of them."

They entered through the gate and the other four bees made sure that the two men saw each one of them flying from one flower to another as they would do normally.

"Well this certainly needs to be something to take into consideration as regards our granting of planning permission to build houses on this site," one of the council men stated.

"Yes, you are right. These bees look like they are a rare or endangered species or even an undiscovered species, and that means that they and their habitat would be protected by law."

"I think we have seen enough, we should go back to the office. Then we can make our report, and ask the council expert on bees to come along to the meadow. Maybe he can identify or perhaps even capture one."

Bea heard this last sentence and became of course very nervous. If someone caught one of the red bees, they would soon realise that it was just red pollen, and the whole plan would come to nothing. Once the two men had left, the six red bees regrouped at their hiding place, to wait for the next people to arrive. Bea explained to the others that they must be very careful from now on as one of the council men had mentioned someone coming to identify and possibly catch one of them.

Later that day, another man arrived, the council expert on bees, and he brought with him a large net. A bee on duty at the gate related all this to Bea. She was concerned, up until this point it had been just a game, but now they all needed to be extremely alert if they were to convince the man without getting caught. Bea devised a plan that involved the six red bees working in pairs. If the bee expert looked like he was about to catch one of the bees in his net, the other bee must fly very close to him and put him off what he was doing.

The bee expert was talking to Jessica and David, the two campers, when the six bees arrived. As soon as the bees were sure that he had seen them they divided up into their groups and kept their distance by visiting different flowers. The man took a notebook and pencil out of his pocket and started to scribble something down. Bea and Amelia made sure that Jessica and David saw them as well.

"Look over there," Jessica said to the man, "there are another two bees on those flowers."

"Yes, I see them, they are fascinating," he replied.

The council bee expert made some more notes as he watched Bea and Amelia. Meanwhile the other two bees that he had been watching moved off to a safer distance. Once he had finished writing, he picked up his net, and started to walk towards Bea and Amelia.

The time had arrived for the two of them to be even more careful. He made a bad attempt at swooping Bea into the net but with a flick of her wings

Bea moved just out of reach. An easy escape she thought to herself. The man went to make a second swoop, and as he did so, Amelia flew very close to him, completely putting him off. Bea moved again. This time he tried to capture Amelia who had by now settled on a rather pretty yellow flower. As the net came rushing towards Amelia it looked as if he might catch her, but Bea bravely flew in front of his eyes and the man missed Amelia and the flower. The six red bees working in pairs flew around him but try as he might he was not able to capture any of them.

Luckily, the bee expert did not hear Bea, Amelia and the others laughing at their little game, he just saw six red bees flying further and further away in different directions while he became hot, bothered and tired trying to catch them. From a safe distance, the bees watched him search around for them. All he found was their friends from the hive, and there was no point in capturing a normal looking yellow and black bee. Finally, exhausted he flopped down on the grass with Jessica and David and started to talk to them again.

"This is all very exciting for me," he puffed, getting his breath back.

"Why's that?" asked Jessica watching him scribble some more notes.

"Well," he replied, "we have never had anything like this before in this area. I expect that the government might want to carry out a full scientific survey of this place and the surrounding land. That is what my report will recommend."

"Will that stop the developers building on the meadow?" she asked.

"It certainly would!" chuckled the man.

"Wouldn't the developers become angry if that were the case?" David enquired.

"Yes, I expect so," replied the bee expert, "but the law is the law and we all have to respect it. I'm finished here for the day so I'll say goodbye and maybe see you again if you are not leaving too soon."

"Yes, we have decided to stay a bit longer just to see what happens," Jessica replied.

The bee expert said "Goodbye", walked back to his council van and drove off. Later in the day, there were more visitors, mostly walkers, some with their dogs, so Bea's team flew again. Curiously though, despite their best efforts nobody seemed to notice them. Perhaps they had not heard the news about the red bees yet.

Part 5

Next morning, Bea gathered her teams in the hive and they went over their

plan for the day under the Queen's watchful gaze. There was still no news

from any of the other creatures about any species of plant, tree, bird,

animal, insect, fish or even an amphibian being very special. So the plan

was going to be similar to the day before. The yellow team of normal

looking messenger bees would fly out and watch for anyone coming into

the meadow. The red team, as they had become known, would fly down to

the red flowers, don their disguises, and wait to be told when to put on their

performance.

"Good luck to all of you," the Queen said waving, "and be very careful not

to get caught."

"But of course!" smiled Bea looking back towards the Queen.

Proudly, the red and yellow teams flew from the hive in close formation,

and did some acrobatics just for the Queen and the other watching bees as

they left.

"I do hope they take getting caught a bit more seriously," said a frowning

Wise Old Bee. "If one of the disguised bees is captured, we are back to where we started, and may have to move very quickly if we are to survive."

"Yes, I hope so too," a worried Queen replied.

The red team prepared themselves and waited for news to arrive from the yellow team at the gate just as they had done the day before. For good measure, Bea flew to the tent, to let Jessica and David know that the red bees were still about and then returned to her group and waited with the others. The morning wore on. Stephanie, once again on duty at the gate, brought the team news of the arrival of two unsavoury looking characters.

"I think you should be very careful with these two as they don't look like the other nice visitors that come here, they look sinister and suspicious to me," she warned Bea.

"Thank you Stephanie. OK, red team, let's all go and be seen but keep your distance," said Bea.

The red team flew in the direction of the gate and there they found the two men talking about the meadow and the building of houses on it. Bea and the others listened carefully to their conversation.

"This has already cost us a lot of money, I can't believe how much we have spent on this project," one developer said grumpily.

"Not only that but all that profit in those houses we want to build will be lost as well," replied the other in a very irate tone.

"What a fuss about some overgrown field, perhaps we should just plough it up like we did that last place we built on," the first developer said with a nasty grin on his face.

What they did not realise was that not only had the bees heard them, but their conversation had also been heard by Jessica. She had been looking at flowers and checking their names and details in a guide book that she had brought on holiday with her. When the two shady looking characters started talking, she was behind the hedge that bordered the meadow and able to hear the conversation. When she had heard enough she crept away so as not to be seen by the two men talking outside.

When Jessica arrived back at the tent she told David all about what she had overheard. They discussed what they could do to stop these men from tearing the meadow apart before the red species of bees could be investigated. Meanwhile, Bea and one of her team had been spotted by the dubious looking developers.

"Look Frank, there's two of those red bees, let's try and grab one of them."

"What with, Pete, you know that they can sting don't you?"

"Well it is worth a go."

The two men entered through the gate and started to chase the two bees. The other four members of the red team soon joined Bea and Sophie who then led the pair a merry dance. The two developers were very unfit and becoming weary and beginning to give up. Seeing this made Bea a bit too brave and for a brief moment she landed on one of them. A little of the red pollen came off her and went on the developer's shirt. Bea tried to remove it, but she did not have enough time and her contact with the man left a small red mark. The two men gave up chasing the bees and trudged back, panting and grumbling, towards the entrance. Then one of them noticed the red mark on the other's shirt.

"Wait a minute Pete; you have a red mark on your shirt."

"Do I Frank?" Pete replied.

'Yes, did one of the bees touch you?"

"I don't think so, I never felt anything."

"Hmmm," Frank said, "I think that there may be more to this than meets the eye. Perhaps we ought to just bulldoze the place like we said and plead ignorance if anyone says anything or complains."

"That sounds alright to me," Pete replied, laughing loudly.

The two developers got into a large black luxury car with dark windows and drove off quickly. Meanwhile David and Jessica searched the internet for any news about the red bees. They found a headline about the meadow, it read:

"Local Meadow To Undergo Full Scientific Survey"

"That's great news," exclaimed Jessica, "this beautiful place will be protected. With this discovery they won't be able to build houses here."

"I don't trust those two developers and I think that we should call that green group that organises protests just in case."

"That's a good idea because they might try something before the survey can be completed," said Jessica.

David searched on his phone for the green group's number and called it.

"Hello, is that the Friends of the Trees?" he enquired.

"Yes, it is, how can we help you?" a man replied.

"Have you heard about the scientific study about to take place in Old Oak meadow?"

"Yes, we have, it seems to be very interesting."

"Well, I'm camping in Old Oak with my girlfriend and she overheard some developers talking. It sounded as if they are planning to bulldoze and dig it up before the survey can take place. Can you send some of your group down to help us stop them?"

"Oh my goodness, yes certainly, let me make some telephone calls and we can ask some of our staff and volunteers to come down to help out."

"OK, but hurry, we are on our own."

"I don't trust those developers either," said Jessica when David had finished the call, "they didn't seem to be very honest."

"I'm sure some staff and volunteers from Friends of the Trees will arrive soon but until then it is going to be up to us if the developers return."

Later that same day, four young people did indeed arrive on bicycles, loaded down with camping equipment. Stephanie once again went off to tell Bea about their arrival. By the time the red team found them the four were unpacking and talking to David and Jessica.

"We are the first group from Friends of the Trees, and I'm Tom" said a young man introducing himself, "others are coming, but maybe not until tomorrow."

"Until then," said a young woman called Charlotte, "we need to spread ourselves out so we can keep a lookout for those developers. We have dealt with these sorts of people before and they are very sneaky. They won't wait to see if they get the planning permission approved. They will just destroy the meadow and then it won't be worth saving."

"Look!" said Jessica, "There are some of those red bees we saw and photographed."

"Wow!" said the new arrivals, almost in unison and all very impressed.

The red team carried out their usual display, making sure that everyone saw them, before Bea led them off. After cleaning off the pollen they returned to the hive as yellow bees. They had a lot to talk about and discuss when they arrived. In the meadow the group from Friends of the Trees put up two tents, some distance from Jessica and David's, but still close enough to call for help if anything occurred during the night.

It was sometime later that the John the reporter and Ben the photographer from the local newspaper returned. They were surprised to see the new arrivals from Friends of the Trees who had joined the couple on holiday. Jessica and David told them about Jessica overhearing what the developers had said and explained that because of this they had called Friends of the Trees. John and Ben took a great interest in hearing this news as it was beginning to sound like a very interesting story for the local newspaper. John interviewed David, Jessica and the four individuals from Friends of the Trees, while Ben took a large number of photographs of them, the meadow and the tents.

"Why have you come to Old Oak meadow?" the reporter, John, asked.

"We have heard," replied Tom, "that this could be a special place with a unique species in it, and anyway, it is still a beautiful place even if there aren't any rare species of animal or plant here. These developers want to destroy our countryside to build houses on it when there is plenty of land in the towns and cities that could and needs to be re-developed."

"Why do you think they do that?" enquired John.

"Because it is more expensive and difficult to re-develop old town and city sites and they can make more money ripping up our beautiful open spaces."

"It is pure greed as always and trying to maximise profit," explained

Charlotte, the spokesperson for Friends of the Trees. "Also, if we keep building away from our main towns and cities, we encourage more private car use and that means never meeting the necessary commitments to stop climate change. If we don't act now our children will have to deal with our failure to have done so."

"Thank you for your comments;" said John, "you and Old Oak are going to be the headline story on our website this evening and in the newspaper tomorrow."

After they had finished the interview John and Ben left to write up their story. In the hive all the bees were waiting keenly to hear from Bea and her team. They all gathered around them on their return. Bea recounted to them all the events that had taken place, especially that the developers might come and destroy the meadow, with or without permission. She also said that there were some people camping and trying to stop this from happening. An eerie silence followed when she had finished speaking. At first nobody wanted to speak.

"We have another problem," said the Wise Old Bee, "there are not many of those red flowers and they are beginning to stop flowering, which means an end to the red pollen for your disguise."

"And as yet we still haven't identified a species to replace the red bee story," added the Queen.

"What can we do about that?" asked a crestfallen looking Bea.

"We need to collect as much of the red pollen as we can," the Wise Old Bee answered, "a team can bring it back here, even though it is more dangerous, and we can then store and use it carefully. We must try and brush as much off as we can when you return to the hive each time you fly."

"If we do that we risk the red bees being seen entering the hive," the Queen pointed out worriedly.

"That's a chance that we must now take," replied the Wise Old Bee.

"Yes agreed, we will also need more than just our red bee act, in case the developers come to destroy the meadow," Bea stated forcefully.

"Yes, we will and we can," the Wise Old Bee answered, "we need to talk to the wasps, mosquitoes, birds, animals and any other creatures that bite, dig, scratch and can throw things and ask them to help us protect our home. It is time for every inhabitant of our beloved meadow to cooperate and fight together to save it. But all the creatures must be told that there are people in the meadow trying to help us save it and that we should try to help them. Nobody is to be harmed in the saving of our home. The intention is only to scare the developers away."

"I'm sure the birds, ants, mosquitoes, squirrels, badgers, moles, hedgehogs and other creatures can help us and will understand that. Nearly everyone will want to join us but the wasps have never been very helpful and we really could do with them fighting alongside us," said the Queen.

"I know that you don't fly very often Queen Bee but in this case I think that a visit to the wasp nest by you may help us to persuade them," suggested the Wise Old Bee.

"Yes, of course, not a pleasant task but a very necessary one," replied the Queen, "Stephanie, please take as many of the bees as you need and tell all the mosquitoes, ants, birds, animals and any other creatures that you can find, that we need their help. We shall need to organise everyone into the first and second lines of defence so that we can best protect our home. Wise Old Bee, please organise the collection of as much red pollen as possible and bring it back here to the hive. I will take Bea and some of the red team to try and persuade the wasps that it is in their best interests to help us."

It was now early evening but as it was midsummer there remained enough light for the bees to fly. They organised themselves and left the hive on their different missions. The Queen, Bea, and two others from her team, flew to a quiet corner of the meadow where there was a large and ominous looking wasp nest. The bees rarely got on with the wasps and there was often some bad feelings between the two. None of the inhabitants of the meadow for that matter liked to go near the wasp nest. They were not very popular with anyone. When the four bees arrived there did not appear to be

any wasps at home.

"We will just have to wait for them to return," said the Queen.

"I don't like it," replied a nervous Bea, "it is far too quiet."

Suddenly, they were surrounded by a large number of wasps. Bea looked

even more nervous; the wasps always reacted in this way. They ganged up

on everyone that came near them and they looked very menacing.

"What do you want?" a rather large wasp rasped at the Queen.

"Are you in charge?" the Queen replied, her voice faltering just a little.

"That depends on what you want," the wasp replied in a deep and disconcerting voice.

"We need your help in trying to stop the destruction of the meadow and some people building houses on it," replied the Queen, sounding less shaky now, her confidence growing because of the seriousness of their visit.

The Queen and Bea explained all the events that had led up to their coming to ask the wasps for their help. She explained that every other creature was being asked, but they really needed the wasps' help the most. On hearing the story, the large wasp replied.

"Why should we care if they rip this place up and build houses on it? We like houses as we can build good nests in the lofts, garages and walls. We like their sheds as well."

"I know you do and can," replied the Queen, "but when your nests are discovered they are sprayed with chemicals to make you leave. Do you really want to be made homeless like that?"

"We need to think about this, we shall let you know tomorrow," came the response.

It was time to leave. The bees had done all that they could to persuade the wasps and they made their way back to the hive, tired from their long day.

By the time they reached home all of the other bees had returned too.

The assigned team had collected as much of the red pollen as possible and stored it in the hive. All the colonies of ants had immediately agreed to help, as had all the mosquitoes and the birds. The squirrels, as soon as they had been asked, had cheerfully retrieved all of their acorns and horse chestnuts to provide ammunition. Bees had flown far and wide across the meadow and arrived back at the hive with offers of help. The moles, rabbits and the badgers had all been contacted and had promised the bees to collaborate by digging out the ground wherever necessary to try to stop the developers. The foxes had also agreed to help with digging and being on guard. The hedgehogs pledged to do what they could even though they moved quite slowly. Help from all creatures no matter how large or small was being volunteered to protect the home they shared. Even the swans, who sometimes appeared quite aloof, had volunteered to be on guard and raise the alarm if the developers tried to enter the meadow. They could also chase them out if they were called upon to do so. The fish, frogs, newts and others could not see how they could help but said that they would think of something if the developers reached the stream. A beautiful sunset closed the day in the meadow and all the living creatures in it hoped that they could save their home as they settled down for the night.

Part 6

The next morning the bees were again greeted with a blue sky and the start of another sunny day. Bea, as usual, zoomed out of the hive first and checked to see that everything was alright in the meadow. She found that more tents were being set up, along with banners flying in the light breeze that read, "Save the Trees" and others "Save the Meadow".

Bea saw mostly young people wearing very casual clothes, jeans, shorts and T-shirts; some had brought guitars with them. Later on another small group of three individuals arrived, looking a bit more smartly dressed. Their tent looked larger and more professional with "Field Research Team" written on it. This was clearly the research team of scientists and they were soon joined by the local council bee expert who returned to help them with their work.

Bea flew back to the hive. Here she found a delegation from the wasps who had agreed to help on this occasion, reluctantly, they added. Everyone knew that the wasps could be a bit grumpy and difficult to deal with. The Queen gave them strict instructions not to attack the growing number of people that had arrived, who had come here just to try to protect Old Oak. After the wasps had gone the Queen sighed, hoping that they had understood, as to who were friends and who were the enemy.

"I hope I got through to them," she told the assembled bees.

"We must keep an eye on them as they can be very difficult," replied the Wise Old Bee.

"What news do you have Bea?" the Queen asked.

"A group of scientists have arrived so hopefully we can count on them to find a really rare or endangered species. We should at least try to show them the red bees in case they don't find anything else."

"You must take extra care not to get caught by these people as they are professionals. So don't make any mistakes or get too close," the Wise Old Bee said with as much seniority as she could.

"We will be extra careful Wise Old Bee," said Bea, "None of us wants to be captured. Also, there are many more people here now besides the scientists. We have a lot more new friends who have come to help us."

After the meeting most of the bees went back to their usual work while Stephanie's yellow team kept watch on events as they unfolded during the day. Because of the limited supply of red pollen, only Bea and three of her team disguised themselves using as little of it as they could. They would not be able to make many more flights in disguise that day, so they had to make every flight count to convince the new visitors that they were indeed special. When they were ready, Bea led them to the tents of the scientists and those of Friends of The Trees and they made their display so as to be noticed. The new arrivals from Friends of the Trees were very impressed. One of the scientists, on spying a red bee shouted out.

"Quick, where are the nets? We need to capture one of those red bees!"

The other two scientists and the council bee expert hastily picked up some nets and the four of them set off in pursuit. Bea and the other red bees had become expert at this game of avoiding the nets by now. After a few swipes that came nowhere near them, the bees broke formation and flew off in different directions. When neither the scientists nor the bee expert could see any more red bees, they went back to their work of collecting samples and looking at all sorts of plants, insects, birds, aquatic and animal life. The four bees returned to the hive and shook and brushed off as much of the pollen as possible to save it for the next flight should they need to use it. The amount of red pollen remaining had become very low.

Back at the encampment, some of the people were standing around and looking at their phones and tablets. The website of the local newspaper had caught their attention. Today's headline read:

"Green Group Fights To Save Unique Meadow From Greedy Developers"

At the gate of the meadow a different conversation was taking place. The two suspicious looking developers, Frank and Pete, had arrived along with a councillor from the local council.

"I thought you said that this planning permission was just a formality," Frank said angrily to the councillor.

"Yes, didn't we pay you enough money to make sure that it went through without any problems?" demanded Pete.

"Have you seen the story on the internet and in the local paper?" Frank continued.

"Yes, I have. How was I to know that all this was going to happen? We will have to get rid of those red bees somehow," the councillor replied.

"And what about all this lot?" Frank said pointing at all of the tents; "This will be on national TV soon and all over social media."

"Perhaps, we should do it our way," Pete said with an evil grin as he spoke the words.

"I don't want to see any violence," the councillor replied, "once the scientists have gone we can have these protestors removed legally."

"But that takes time," Frank replied, "and time as you know costs money, our money."

At that moment the local reporter John and the photographer Ben arrived.

"Gentlemen," said John addressing all three, "just the people I wanted to ask about their side of the story."

"No comment," replied the councillor.

"Councillor, how nice to see you working with our local developers for the benefit of all in the local community," said John in a slightly sarcastic tone.

"No comment," the councillor repeated more forcefully.

"How about you good citizens?" John asked turning to Pete and Frank.

"Like he said," Frank replied in a gruff voice, "no comment."

"Thank you gentlemen, you have been most uncooperative," said John, over his shoulder as he walked away with Ben.

They entered through the gate to take photographs and interview more of the new arrivals from Friends of the Trees. They also talked to the scientists to find out if they had discovered anything interesting. The scientists hinted that they might be on the trail of something, but they declined to say what it was until they could confirm their findings.

By midday, it seemed as if all the people from Friends of the Trees who were going to come had now arrived. Those that had arrived during the morning had set up their tents and their defences, along with the others, should there to be an attempt by the developers to try and make them leave.

At the hive the bees decided to use what might be the last of the red pollen to make as many of the new arrivals as possible, some of whom may not have seen them earlier that day, believe in their existence. Once more Bea, and her team of bees, left the hive disguised in red and flew about the tents making themselves as visible as could be. The Friends of the Trees volunteers were very impressed; it made them think that the meadow was even more special than just being a pretty part of the countryside. The bees did not have to worry about getting caught this time as the scientists and bee expert were not around when they put on their display. They could be found collecting samples elsewhere.

Once they returned to the hive, the bees removed as before, as much of the red pollen as they could just in case they needed to fly again as the red team. There was even less now and it may not have been enough for more than two or three of the team to fly disguised.

Nothing much else seemed to happen that day. The group from Friends of the Trees sat around playing card and ball games, strumming their guitars and singing songs. Meanwhile the scientists and the local bee expert carried on with their research. People arrived from the nearby village, some to walk their dogs, others just to see what was happening because of all the stories now on the internet and in the local newspaper that they had read about. The bees decided not to make another flight that day in disguise as everybody seemed to be convinced of their existence.

Everyone in the encampment appeared quite relaxed, apart from the scientists who had returned to their tent very excited. They had split up earlier in the day and had been covering as much of the meadow as they could. Now they had developed a theory that they wanted to explore.

Another beautiful sunset ended the day in the meadow. That evening there was a lot of noise around the small cooking stoves to accompany the sounds of the insects, animals and the birds.

A glorious morning greeted the bees the next day as they went about their daily work as did all the other creatures. Apart from those assigned to guard duty or preparing to defend the meadow. The scientists and bee expert continued to work in different parts of it. A few of the protestors from Friends of the Trees went off to buy newspapers to confirm what they were seeing on the internet. One headline read:

"Scientists On Trail Of Unique Species. Is It The Red Bees Or Something Else?"

In a nearby town the same headline had been read by the unsavoury developers. They were not very happy about what they saw and decided to make plans on what to do next.

"We had better do this our way then Pete," said Frank, "you talk to the security guys and I'll contact the lads with the heavy equipment."
"Yeah, we'll remove these green protestors and then tear the place apart. That way it will only be fit for building on, there will be nothing left of their precious field by the time we have finished with it," Pete replied.

They both laughed out loud thinking about what they planned to do early the next day.

Part 7

The next day, Bea woke even earlier, prepared herself and when she could not wait any longer left the hive. Outside she heard a lot of noise and commotion unlike anything that she had heard before. It was the foxes and the swans howling, honking, screeching and generally making a lot of noise in the distance. True to their word they were giving the first alarm signal of the coming danger. Near the gate, one of the volunteers from Friends of the Trees came running back towards the tents, shouting for everyone to get up and prepare themselves. The sun had not yet risen very far. Bea zoomed off in the direction that the excited man had come from.

Thundering down the road several heavy plant machines appeared, bulldozers and excavators, the sort that could rip the meadow to shreds in a short space of time. Two coaches full of people had arrived. Some of them were already standing outside talking on their mobile phones. They all had 'SECURITY' written on the back of their black jackets. They did not look very nice at all. Bea quickly darted back to the hive, the battle for the meadow was about to begin.

She quickly told her news and updated all the other bees. The Queen ordered a small group to go and tell the wasps and mosquitoes to be ready since they were the first line of defence against these men and their bulldozers and excavators. Others she dispatched to tell the birds, the animals, the ants and other insects to be prepared. She asked another bee to tell the cows to be on standby in case any developers were able to get into the meadow and needed to be herded out again.

The bees hoped that this would be enough to save their home. The group from Friends of the Trees along with Jessica and David were busy chaining themselves to the gate, to each other, and to the trees. Everything was ready. Bea made her way back to the gate to observe the front line of defences. Most of the other bees followed her. They could not do anything more, as honey bees could only sting once, and they died if they did. Now it was up to all their friends to protect their home. Their work was done.

In the distance, the heavy plant machines lumbered towards the entrance of the meadow. Pete and Frank, surrounded by a group of security men stood by the gate.

Frank shouted loudly, "We can do this the easy way or the hard way, either way, you will be leaving today."

"Not without a court order," one of the protestors responded.

"Suit yourself, that's your choice to make" replied Frank.

He raised his hand in the air to give the signal to start and several security guards stepped forward with bolt cutters to cut the chains securing the people to the gate. As they did a loud buzzing sound could be heard. Before they had a chance to cut any of the chains the wasps appeared, in a large angry cloud, and started their attack on them. A swarm of mosquitoes, making up the rest of the first line of defence, quickly followed the wasps. These men dropped their tools as they had all been stung and bitten several times and the stinging and biting only stopped when they ran away from the gate. Bea thought that she could almost hear the wasps and mosquitoes laughing as they pursued and stung and bit the security guards.

Several other guards picked up the tools, and before the wasps and mosquitoes had time to regroup, they managed to cut the chains of the volunteers attached to the gate. They were pushed roughly aside; Frank and Pete laughed as they walked through the gate and into the meadow. They did not laugh for long, as the squirrels hiding in the trees, launched the second wave of defence. A hail of acorns and horse chestnuts rained down on the men that had entered through the gate. This was quickly followed by many birds, both large and small, that flew above and attacked them by dropping stones onto their heads.

One of the bulldozers moved forward and entered by knocking the gate off its hinges. It was beginning to look like nothing could stop the machines. But suddenly the whole bulldozer sank into a deep hole that the hardworking moles, rabbits, badgers and foxes had made under the ground. It could not go forwards or backwards. Perplexed, the driver climbed down from his cab. As he did so he removed one of his boots as something was biting his foot. A small group of ants wisely decided that this was the best time to run away. As he brought his foot down to stamp on them, he stood on some prickly hedgehogs who had rushed to their rescue. He was last seen hopping away pursued by a group of swans.

The wasps and mosquitoes had now regrouped and they attacked a second time. There seemed to be countless numbers of them and soon Frank, Pete and the security men were forced to leave. Frank thought it strange that only he, Pete, the machine operators and their security team were being attacked. Very bizarre! From outside and still being stung and bitten, Frank raised his hand again, a signal for the rest of the heavy machines to enter into the meadow and start ploughing it up, but nothing happened. There were no sounds of heavy machines starting and moving. As he looked around, he could see why.

The drivers of the bulldozers and excavators could be seen jumping up and down or getting out of the cabs as quickly as they could. Whilst they had been parked up, the armies of ants had crept up on them and the drivers now found them in their clothes, shoes and in their hair. Mosquitoes and wasps buzzed close to the drivers as they got out of their machines and in an instant had bitten and stung them. One man, who had been outside at the time, jumped into what looked like an empty cab to escape the wasps and mosquitoes. He sat on several waiting and prickly hedgehogs, howled loudly and quickly jumped out again rubbing the seat of his trousers. More acorns, horse chestnuts and stones reigned down from the squirrels and the birds. Foxes and swans snapped at the ankles of the drivers. The men could not operate the heavy machines as they had all been bitten, stung and hit so many times. A few of the security men had got into the two coaches and quickly driven away leaving their companions to run away as fast as they could.

It was at this time that several vans and cars arrived; the local and national media had come to look for a story. Bea flew like the wind, from squadron to squadron of wasps and mosquitoes, to quickly tell their leaders that these people, for the moment at least, were friends as well, and not to attack them.

The reporters and cameramen had a great time watching and filming the end of the battle as a group of insects, birds and animals chased away a lot of big grown men. None of them wanted to give any interviews as they were all too busy running away and up the road. However, the Friends of the Trees team, Jessica and David, the scientists and the local bee expert were only too happy to tell their side of the story. All of them were amazed at what they had seen and none of them could explain the orchestrated attacks by all the inhabitants of the meadow. The scientists also added that they expected to have some more exciting news tomorrow for the media, but that they had a bit more work to do today to be sure.

The rest of the day became quiet after the events of the early morning and everyone felt confident that the developers would not come back. The volunteers spent the day sitting around and playing music and games as they waited to see what the scientists had discovered. The national media left thinking that they had the main story covered and went on to look for the next interesting piece of news. John and Ben from the local paper said that they would come back the following day to hear what the scientists had discovered.

The next day started as an uneventful one, where normality returned for the creatures of the meadow and the volunteers had very little to do, apart from wait for the scientists who were getting ready to announce the results of their study. John, the local reporter and Ben the photographer returned to interview the scientists at the allotted hour. They were the only ones from the media to do so. As they did, the group from Friends of the Trees also gathered around the scientists' tent, along with David and Jessica. Unbeknown to any of them, so did several bees, who also wanted to know what the scientists had discovered and what it meant for the meadows' inhabitants. They kept close to the large group of people so that they could hear. The research team's group leader started to speak.

"What we have discovered is a very rare plant with red flowers," said the scientific study leader, "this is what we believe made the bees red. We don't think we have seen any red bees for a day or so and we have found that these plants are no longer producing pollen."

"So how rare are these plants?" asked the reporter.

"They are very rare indeed, it is a combination of the soil and the local habitat, you will only find these plants in a handful of other places around the country."

"So, can we assume then the local council couldn't grant planning permission to build houses here?" asked Charlotte from Friends of the Trees.

"That's correct," replied, the leader, "the government must make this a special reserve, a site of special scientific interest."

"That's very good news," stated Charlotte.

"Great," said John, "I'll write all this up for tomorrow's headline and place it on our website later today. It looks as if I have a national scoop since the rest of the media couldn't wait for a day or two."

John and Ben left, and later the scientists packed up their tent and equipment and did the same, along with the local bee expert. Bea and the other bees flew around the meadow telling all the other creatures, about how it seemed as if their home had been saved. All because of the red flower that Bea had first thought of using as a disguise! The bees made sure that everyone knew, if it was not known already, that it was only through the cooperation of all of them, including the wasps, that they had saved their home.

Bea woke up more impatient than usual the next day. The sun had risen but none of the Friends of the Trees group or the camping couple seemed to be in any hurry to do so. When they eventually did gather together they started to prepare breakfast. Some looked at their phones and tablets. One of them read out a headline and a very loud "Hooray" could be heard. Bea read the headline too:

"Rare Species Of Plant Found In Old Oak Meadow. Planning Permission Is Refused"

Further down the page, there was more related news. In the next article, John the reporter had written about how two developers and a councillor, were being interviewed by the police, who were expected to press charges on all three of them before the end of the day. John had added that he believed that the developers had tried to influence the council and that they may have paid money to help push through the planning permission. This of course would be illegal if it had indeed taken place.

The inhabitants of the meadow had won! Later that day, the group from Friends of the Trees along with David and Jessica held a big party. There was much to celebrate. Bea went back to the hive to tell everyone about the news. Because of the noise at the party the volunteers and campers were having, it could not be heard, but in the background, if you listened very carefully, you could hear all the creatures of the meadow having a buzz of a party too.

The End

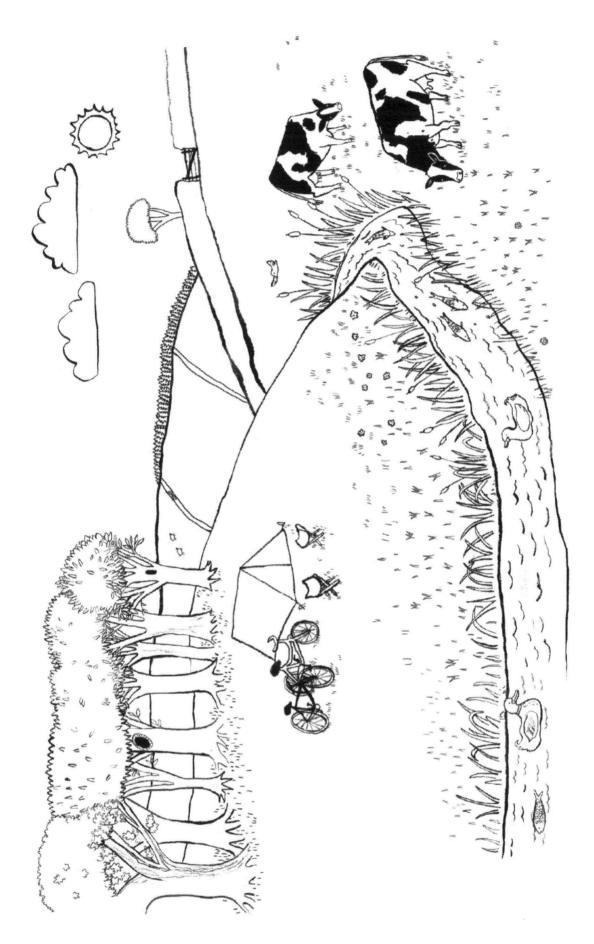

Campers in the meadow

This page intentionally left blank

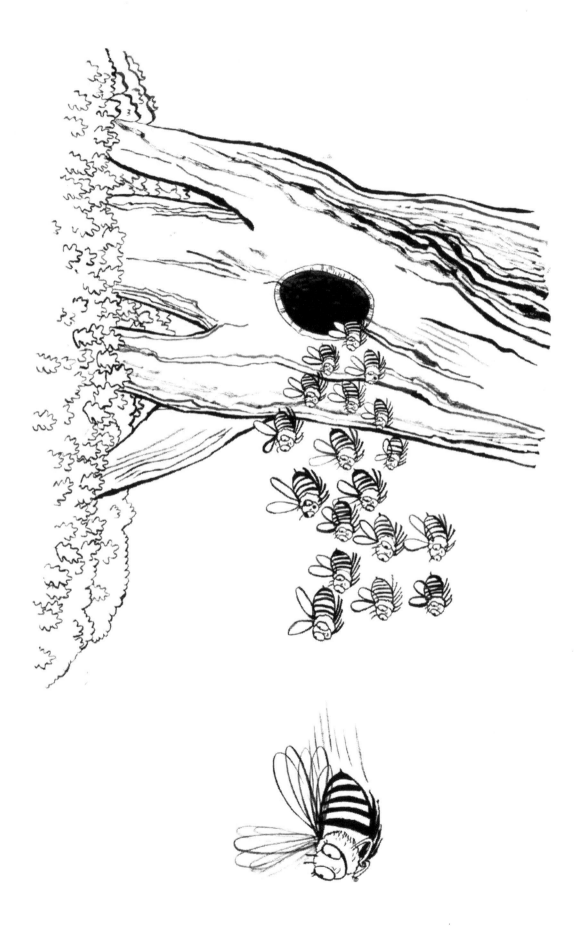

Zooming out of the hive

This page intentionally left blank

SITE NOTICE

PLANNING PERMISSION

JOB NUMBER	99008347777777829917824738402387408 7
DESCRIPTION	Planning permission sought to destroy all and build 600, six bedroom eco homes for families.
LOCATION	The Meadow
DATE	ASAP

A copy of the application can be found online at, www.countyc.gov.uk/environment/building/houses/planning/planning-permissions/plans/pdf/unaffordablehousing//. All objections mus be submitted and sent to the planning office by November. affordable housing will be provided on this site, a total of 1.5 1 bedroom houses will be available to rent or buy.

Any other objections must be placed in writing and sent to PO BOX 1989787878.

ARTIST IMPRESSION

A new notice – Planning permission?

This page intentionally left blank

An audience with the queen

This page intentionally left blank

Bea flies around Jessica and David

This page intentionally left blank

The men from the council arrive

This page intentionally left blank

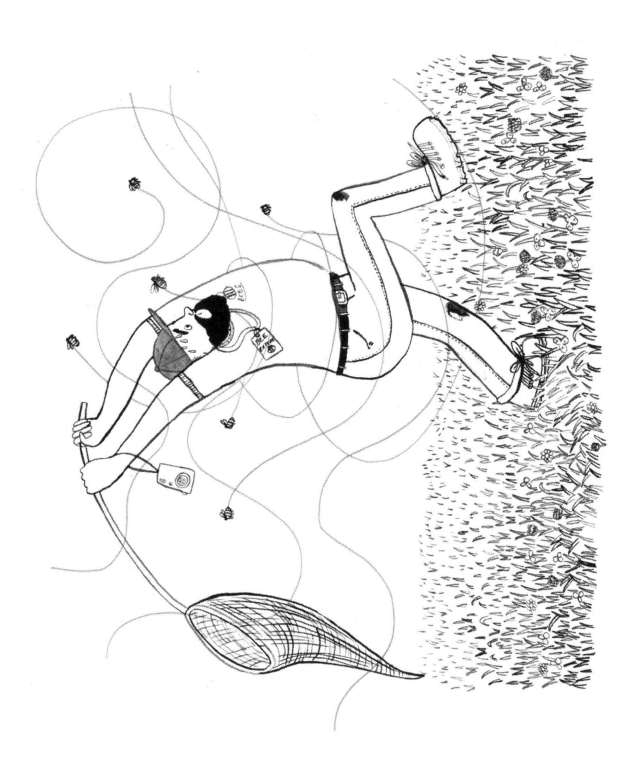

The bee expert tries to capture a red bee

This page intentionally left blank

Two dubious looking developers

This page intentionally left blank

A meeting with the wasps

This page intentionally left blank

Friends of the trees set up camp

This page intentionally left blank

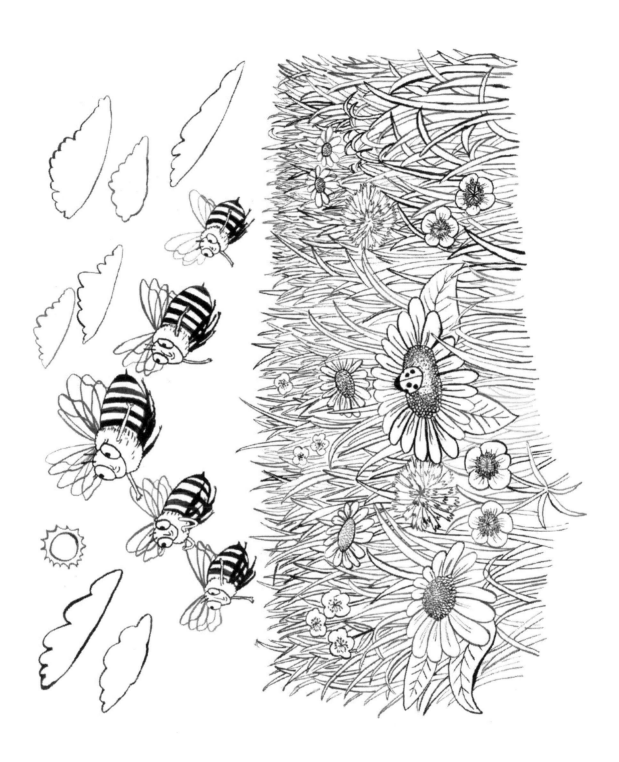

Formation flying of the red bees

This page intentionally left blank

A bulldozer falls into a trap

This page intentionally left blank

A buzz of a party

26963457R10054

Printed in Great Britain
by Amazon